The Sweet Treats Lesson

Written by
A.Q. Saghail

Illustrated with
MidJourney

Sweetville.

The town was known for having many different kinds of
sweets and treats.

From cakes and cookies to muffins, ice creams,
and lollies.

The kids in Sweetville had a favorite pastime.

Each morning, they strolled down the street to the
bakery to grab their favorite sweets or treats.

It was the highlight of their day.

But there was one tiny problem.

They loved munching so much that they forgot
the rubbish they left behind.

One day, a wizard named Arthur happened to pass through the town of Sweetville.

To his surprise, the beloved town was now so messy.

There was rubbish everywhere.

Arthur was not happy upon seeing this mess.

He decided it was time to teach this town a lesson.

The wizard made his way to the middle of the
town and cast a spell with his magic wand.

A spell that for every piece of rubbish thrown in
the wrong place, a sweet or treat will
vanish from the beloved town.

The next day, everything seemed fine at first.
People went on with their day, unaware of
the magic at work.

But then, something happened.

The shelves in the stores began to turn sparse.

Cakes, cookies, and muffins started disappearing
from bakeries, and candies went missing
from candy jars.

The kids were left confused.

What was happening? Where had all our cakes
and muffins gone? They wondered.

Even the parents and bakers scratched their
heads in confusion.

After a few more days, nothing was on the shelves.

All the bakeries in the town were sweet and treat-less.

There were no cookies, cakes, pies, or ice cream.

Everyone in the town gathered together and started
searching for answers.

They searched all over the city for hours and
hours but found no clues.

The children started to feel sad.

As all their hopes faded, they decided to give
up and head home.

But among them, a boy raised his hand.
His name was Tom.

Tom, the boy with a sharp mind, had documented
the strange events.
He noted that sweets vanished whenever wrappers
or rubbish were left lying around.

He also knew about a wizard who lived in the hills.

The wizard hated seeing litter everywhere.

Everyone gathered around Tom as he told them
everything he knew and noticed about
the sweet treats' disappearance.

After listening to Tom, the townsfolk realized they might be the cause of their problem.

Tom suggested they clean up the town, hoping the wizard would forgive them and bring back everything.

And, so it began.

Armed with bags, they started collecting
rubbish around the town and their
neighborhoods.

While they were cleaning up the place, the wizard
watched from a distance.

He was pleased with their hard work.

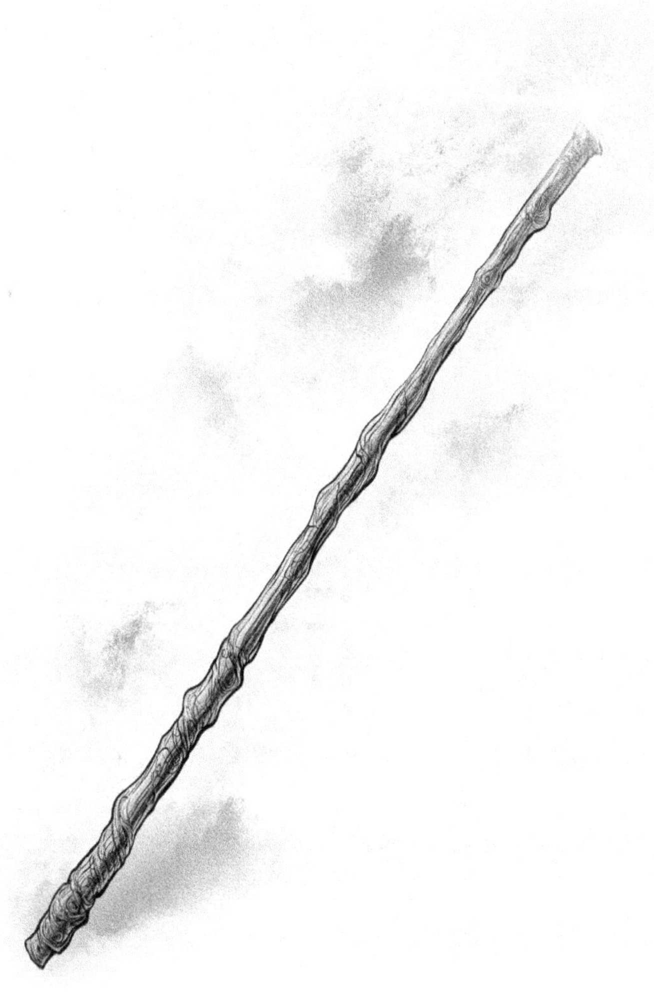

And with his magic wand, he undid the spell.

As noon drew nearer, everyone threw away the last
rubbish bags and returned home.

While returning, they bumped into the sweet smell
of freshly baked muffins and cake.
The sweet aroma was coming from the direction
of their homes.

With smiles, they ran back home to see what was
happening.

They were surprised that sweets and treats filled their
homes as a reward for their hard work.

The kids were happy, and thankful for
the reward.

And once again, the shelves filled to the top.

Everyone thanked their hero, Tom, for his clever
thinking and leadership.
But more importantly, they learned the sweet and
treat lesson.

And so, everything was back to normal.

Sweets and treats returned,
The rubbish went into the bin,
And everyone was happy.

The End

HOW LITTERING HARMS HUMANS, ANIMALS, AND THE ENVIRONMENT

1. Harm Animals

Litter can hurt animals.
They might eat it by mistake,
which can make them very sick.

2. Water Pollution

When trash ends up in rivers or oceans,
it makes the water dirty and unsafe for
fish and people.

3. Poisoning

Some litter, like batteries,
leaks chemicals that can poison the
soil and water.

4. Smelly

Litter makes places look and smell bad,
spoiling beautiful parks and beaches.

5. Soil Damage

Litter can prevent plants from growing by
blocking sunlight and water from reaching the soil.

6. Harmful to Health

Litter can attract pests like rats,
which carry diseases that can make people
sick.

7. Harming Ocean Life

Plastic litter in the ocean can be deadly to sea
creatures like turtles and fish, who mistake it for food.

LITTERING HURTS
ANIMALS, MAKES WATER DIRTY, POISONS SOIL,
AND CAN EVEN
STOP PLANTS FROM GROWING.
IT ALSO ATTRACTS
PESTS
THAT SPREAD DISEASES
AND MAKES PARKS AND BEACHES
SMELLY.
IN THE OCEAN,
PLASTIC LITTER CAN HARM
SEA CREATURES LIKE
TURTLES AND FISH.

THAT'S WHY KEEPING OUR PLANET
CLEAN IS SO IMPORTANT.